362.29 Aretha, David.
A
Ecstasy and other party drugs

HOMESTEAD HS MEDIA CENTER
585398

DATE DUE			

DRUGS

ECSTASY AND OTHER PARTY DRUGS

A MyReportLinks.com Book

David Aretha

MyReportLinks.com Books
an imprint of
Enslow Publishers, Inc.
Box 398, 40 Industrial Road
Berkeley Heights, NJ 07922
USA

MyReportLinks.com Books

MyReportLinks.com Books, an imprint of Enslow Publishers, Inc. MyReportLinks® is a registered trademark of Enslow Publishers, Inc.

Copyright © 2005 by Enslow Publishers, Inc.

All rights reserved.

No part of this book may be reproduced by any means without the written permission of the publisher.

Library of Congress Cataloging-in-Publication Data

Aretha, David.
   Ecstasy and other party drugs / David Aretha.
      p. cm.
   Includes bibliographical references and index.
   ISBN 0-7660-5278-8
   1. Designer drugs—Juvenile literature. 2. Ecstasy (Drug)—Juvenile literature.
   3. Raves (Parties)—Juvenile literature. I. Title.
   RM316.A74 2005
   362.29'9—dc22
                                            2004007589

Printed in the United States of America

10 9 8 7 6 5 4 3 2 1

To Our Readers:
Through the purchase of this book, you and your library gain access to the Report Links that specifically back up this book.
The Publisher will provide access to the Report Links that back up this book and will keep these Report Links up to date on www.myreportlinks.com for five years from the book's first publication date.
We have done our best to make sure all Internet addresses in this book were active and appropriate when we went to press. However, the author and the Publisher have no control over, and assume no liability for, the material available on those Internet sites or on other Web sites they may link to.
The usage of the MyReportLinks.com Books Web site is subject to the terms and conditions stated on the Usage Policy Statement on www.myreportlinks.com.
A password may be required to access the Report Links that back up this book. The password is found on the bottom of page 4 of this book.
Any comments or suggestions can be sent by e-mail to comments@myreportlinks.com or to the address on the back cover.

Photo Credits: AP/Wide World Photos, pp. 1, 10; Clipart.com, p. 3 (young men handcuffed); © 1999–2004 NA World Services, Inc., p. 38; Digital Stock Photos: Government and Social Issues, p. 35; Executive Office of the President/Office of National Drug Control Policy, p. 16; Monitoring the Future Study, Office of National Drug Control Policy, p. 41; MyReportLinks.com Books, pp. 4, back cover; Neuroscience for Kids, p. 21; Office of National Drug Control Policy, p. 20; U.S. Department of Health and Human Services/Substance Abuse and Mental Health Services Administration/Office of Applied Studies, p. 14; Photos.com, p. 3 (center burst); U.S. Department of Health and Human Services/The National Institute on Drug Abuse, pp. 18, 23, 37; U.S. Department of Justice/U.S. Drug Enforcement Administration, p. 34; U.S. Drug Enforcement Administration, pp. 3 (pill), 9, 12, 19, 25, 26, 28, 30, 32, 40, 42.

Cover Photo: AP/Wide World Photos

Disclaimer: While the stories of abuse in this book are real, many of the names have been changed.

Report Links 4

Party Drug Facts 9

1. The Death of the Party 10

2. History of Party Drugs 15

3. Effects of Party Drugs 21

4. How Party Drugs Are Made
   and Sold 30

5. Avoiding Party Drugs, Getting Help 36

Glossary 44

Chapter Notes 45

Further Reading 47

Index 48

About MyReportLinks.com Books

MyReportLinks.com Books
Great Books, Great Links, Great for Research!

The Internet sites listed on the next four pages can save you hours of research time. These Internet sites—we call them "Report Links"—are constantly changing, but we keep them up to date on our Web site.

Give it a try! Type http://www.myreportlinks.com into your browser, click on the series title, then the book title, and scroll down to the Report Links listed for this book.

The Report Links will bring you to great source documents, photographs, and illustrations. MyReportLinks.com Books save you time, feature Report Links that are kept up to date, and make report writing easier than ever!

Please see "To Our Readers" on the copyright page for important information about this book, the MyReportLinks.com Web site, and the Report Links that back up this book.

Please enter **DRE1473** if asked for a password.

Tools   Search   Notes   Discuss   MyReportLinks.com Books   Go!

Report Links

The Internet sites described below can be accessed at http://www.myreportlinks.com

▶ Basic Facts About Drugs: Ecstasy
Editor's Choice

Read the American Council for Drug Education's fact sheet on ecstasy. Learn about the short- and long-term effects of the drug and why it is so dangerous to your health.

▶ Ecstasy: MDMA
Editor's Choice

This summary on ecstasy describes the effects of the popular party drug on the body. These include headaches, jaw clenching, dehydration, hyperthermia, and seizures. Also, learn more about the link between ecstasy and brain damage.

▶ Club Drugs
Editor's Choice

At this Web site, information is presented in the form of slide shows, videos, and reports. You will find statistics on drug use and trends. A "Community Drug Alert Bulletin on Club Drugs" is also available on this site.

▶ Gamma Hydroxybutyrate (GHB)
Editor's Choice

Read this overview on the party drug GHB. Also known as a date-rape drug, GHB affects the brain in very dramatic ways, sometimes leading to death. The tragic story of fourteen-year-old Melanie is a must-read.

▶ Rohypnol: ONDCP Fact Sheet
Editor's Choice

Information is provided on the background, effects, scope of use, and availability of rohypnol. Regional observations, drug scheduling, and relevant legislation are also included.

▶ The Death of the Party: All the Rave, GHB's Hazards Go Unheeded
Editor's Choice

Many teenagers that use GHB are unaware of its serious medical consequences, including death. Educate yourself about the dangers of GHB at this Web site.

Any comments? Contact us: **comments@myreportlinks.com**   5

| Back | Forward | Stop | Review | Home | Explore | Favorites | History |

Report Links

The Internet sites described below can be accessed at http://www.myreportlinks.com

▶ Choose Not To Use Drugs
Written for young women and girls, this article provides an overview of drugs and why they are dangerous. Particular attention is given to party drugs, including ecstasy, Rohypnol, and ketamine.

▶ Date Rape Drugs
Rohypnol is odorless and undetectable when dropped in someone's drink. Some take the drug to extend an alcoholic high. Others slip rohypnol into their victims' drinks so that they may have the chance to sexually abuse them. Learn how to protect yourself.

▶ Ecstasy
In the 1990s and early 2000s, ecstasy use became more and more common among young people. Learn more about the physical symptoms of the drug and the dangerous effects it can have on you.

▶ Ecstasy (MDMA)
This fact sheet explains what ecstasy is and what it looks like. It also provides information on how ecstasy is used and what it does to the body.

▶ Ecstasy, Other Club Drugs, & Other Hallucinogens
This survey on the use of ecstasy reports on trends, differences in ecstasy use among youths and young adults, and use of ecstasy and other illicit drugs among youths and young adults.

▶ Ecstasy and Pot: Double the Memory Damage
Researchers found that ecstasy users were 23 percent more likely to have greater long-term memory loss than people who do not use drugs.

▶ Ecstasy May Be Drug of Choice for Those Trying to Cope with Loneliness, Study Finds
Teens and young adults who feel lonely or ill at ease in social settings may turn to ecstasy. This study finds that ecstasy users need help coping with loneliness.

▶ Ecstasy News
Law enforcement officials now see ecstasy as a national crisis. Use has spread to high schools, college campuses, bars, and even junior high schools. Learn more about the ecstasy trade.

Any comments? Contact us: **comments@myreportlinks.com**

Report Links

The Internet sites described below can be accessed at http://www.myreportlinks.com

▶ Flunitrazepam (Rohypnol)
Flunitrazepam, or Rohypnol, is a sedative used primarily in Europe for the short-term treatment of insomnia. Although it is illegal in the United States, young people are using it to get high. Learn more about this dangerous drug.

▶ Gamma Hydroxybutyrate (GHB): ONDCP Fact Sheet
Information is provided on the background, effects, frequence of use, and availability of GHB. Regional observations, scheduling, and legislation are also included.

▶ GHB
Read about the different forms of GHB, how it is used, who uses it, and how much it costs. Another one of the party drugs, GHB is much more serious than most teenagers realize. Find out why.

▶ Ketamine Fast Facts
Read about some of the consequences of using ketamine. There is also a list of common street names used for ketamine.

▶ LSD
LSD is a hallucinogen that affects people differently depending upon the amount taken, the setting in which the drug is used, and the user's personality, mood, and expectations. View a statistical chart displaying LSD use by students.

▶ MDMA (Ecstasy)
Read about what ecstasy looks like, how it is used, who uses ecstasy, and how much it costs. The consequences of this drug can be very serious. Find out what they are at this Web site.

▶ MDMA (Ecstasy): ONDCP Fact Sheet
Information is provided on the background, effects, scope of use, production, and prevention initiatives concerning ecstasy. Regional observations, scheduling, and legislation are also included.

▶ Mentor Foundation
The Mentor Foundation seeks to promote the well-being and health of young people around the world. Included in their mission is to offer information, support, and effective strategies that will prevent children and teens from using drugs.

Any comments? Contact us: **comments@myreportlinks.com**

Report Links

The Internet sites described below can be accessed at http://www.myreportlinks.com

▶ Narcotics Anonymous
Based on the Twelve Step Program, Narcotics Anonymous can be found in over one hundred countries. Follow the links to find worldwide contact and meeting information. Bulletins, reports, and periodicals are also available to the reader.

▶ NIDA Community Drug Alert Bulletin—Club Drugs
Club drugs are currently used by many young people, who are unaware of their effects. You can read more about the most popular ones, including MDMA, GHB, ketamine, methamphetámine, LSD, and Rohypnol.

▶ Partnership for a Drug-Free America
The Partnership for a Drug-Free America focuses its efforts on reducing substance abuse in America. You will find a recent study on teen drug use, an e-newsletter you can sign up for, and stories of real people trying to cope with addiction.

▶ Rape Drug Awareness
Rape drugs, including GHB, Rohypnol, and ketamine, are illegal, and getting caught with them can bring stiff penalties. Information is provided on how to reduce the risk of a drug-facilitated rape.

▶ Rohypnol
Read this summary on Rohypnol, a party drug. Find out what it looks like and the way it affects the brain and behavior.

▶ Safety Advisory Regarding New Club Drug "Molly"
Similar to ecstasy, Molly is an extremely dangerous drug. In large doses, it acts as a hallucinogen. You will also find information on what it looks like and how it affects the body.

▶ Use and Trafficking of Ecstasy: What the United States Is Doing
Ecstasy has become a major problem across the United States. Learn more about what the government is doing about ecstasy.

▶ XTC: Ecstasy Up Close
Real people tragically affected by ecstasy tell their stories. Slide shows, videos, and informative printable materials are available on the site.

Any comments? Contact us: comments@myreportlinks.com

PARTY DRUG FACTS

✘ According to a 2002 survey, an estimated 10.2 million Americans age twelve and older had tried ecstasy at least once in their lifetimes, representing 4.3 percent of the United States population in that age group.

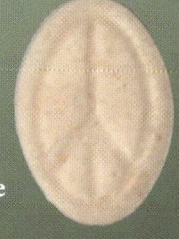

✘ Based on a 2003 study, 3.2 percent of eighth graders and 8.3 percent of twelfth graders had used ecstasy at least once in their lives.

✘ In a 2003 study, one percent of eighth graders and tenth graders reported using Rohypnol at least once during their lifetimes.

✘ Less than 50 percent of tenth graders surveyed in 2003 believed that using ecstasy once or twice was a "great risk."

✘ The number of emergency department mentions of ecstasy increased from 421 in 1995 to 4,026 in 2002. The number of GHB mentions increased from 145 to 3,330 during the same time frame.

✘ As of 2002, the DEA had documented seventy-two deaths relating to GHB and its derivatives.

✘ Approximately 20 percent of all rapes committed in the United States are drug induced.

✘ Ecstasy is illegal in every country in the world due to a United Nations agreement.

✘ The popular party and predatory drugs are illegal in the United States.

✘ From 1996 to 2000, the number of ecstasy tablets seized by the U.S. Drug Enforcement Administration increased from 13,342 to 949,257.

✘ According to federal law, a defendant faces up to a year in prison for first-offense possession of ecstasy, LSD, ketamine, or GHB. First-offense possession of Rohypnol carries a sentence of up to three years.

✘ A defendant could be sentenced to twenty years in prison for trafficking a party drug or predatory drug.

✘ More than 90 percent of teenagers do not take drugs.

Chapter 1 ▶

THE DEATH OF THE PARTY

Seventeen-year-old Nicole* popped her first ecstasy pill at a rave party in Salt Lake City, Utah. A half hour later, the drug "hit me like a tidal wave," she said. "My senses magnified, the lights became more vivid, the music sounded more beautiful, and my new acquaintances felt like best friends."[1] Thus began Nicole's relationship with drugs—one she would continue until lapsing into a coma three months later.

▲ *Young people are attracted to raves because of the bright lights and up-tempo dance music. Ecstasy, ketamine, LSD, and other party drugs can often be found at raves like this one.*

*Disclaimer: While the stories of abuse in this book are real, many of the names have been changed.

Nicole took ecstasy three nights a week. "Only the drug was never as good as the time before," she said.[2] Her eyes became bloodshot, and she was continually sick and depressed. "I began to hate everything," she said. "I hated school, I hated my job, and I fought constantly with my family."[3] Ecstasy could not numb the pain, so she took other drugs.

At a party one night, Nicole sipped from a drink that was laced with GHB (a substance that some people call liquid ecstasy because of its effects). She passed out, and her "friends" dragged her to the bathroom so she could sleep it off. Nicole did not wake up. Eventually, two guys dropped her off at a hospital and left. In the emergency room, Nicole flatlined twice, meaning that her heart had stopped beating. Doctors used defibrillation paddles to save her life, but she fell into a coma.

"Waking up was one of the most horrible experiences of my life," she said. "I awoke in a strange, white room, my ears ringing so loud it was unbearable. Then I began to choke. . . . [The nurses] asked me if I knew where I was, who I was, or what had happened. I shook my head. I knew nothing."[4]

▶ Party and Predatory Drugs

Party drugs, also known as "club drugs" and "rave drugs," emerged at rave parties in the 1980s. They have been ruining young lives ever since. Some party drugs are both stimulants (uppers) and hallucinogens and are taken to achieve a euphoric high. Other party drugs, those known as "predatory drugs" and "date-rape drugs," are depressants. Some people sneak predatory drugs into another person's drink as a means to sedate and rape him or her. More often than not a man slips the drug in a woman's drink. The popular party and predatory drugs are illegal in every state in the United States.

Most party drugs are smuggled into the United States. Some of them, called designer drugs, are made illegally in makeshift laboratories. Because designer drugs are illegal, they are not regulated by government agencies. Thus, no one ever knows about their potency or hazards. Users risk their lives every time they pop a pill.

▶ Many Drugs, Many Dangers

"Party drugs" is a broad term that includes numerous drugs. The most popular are:

- MDMA *(ecstasy)*, 3,4–methylenedioxymethamphetamine
- Ketamine *(special K)*
- LSD *(acid)*, lysergic acid diethylamide
- GHB *(liquid ecstasy)*, gamma hydroxybutyrate
- Rohypnol *(roofies)*, flunitrazepam

Party drugs also include methamphetamine (meth, ice, chalk), amyl nitrate, gamma butyrolactone (GBL), 1,4 butanediol (BD), gamma-hydroxyvalerate (GHV), and many others including

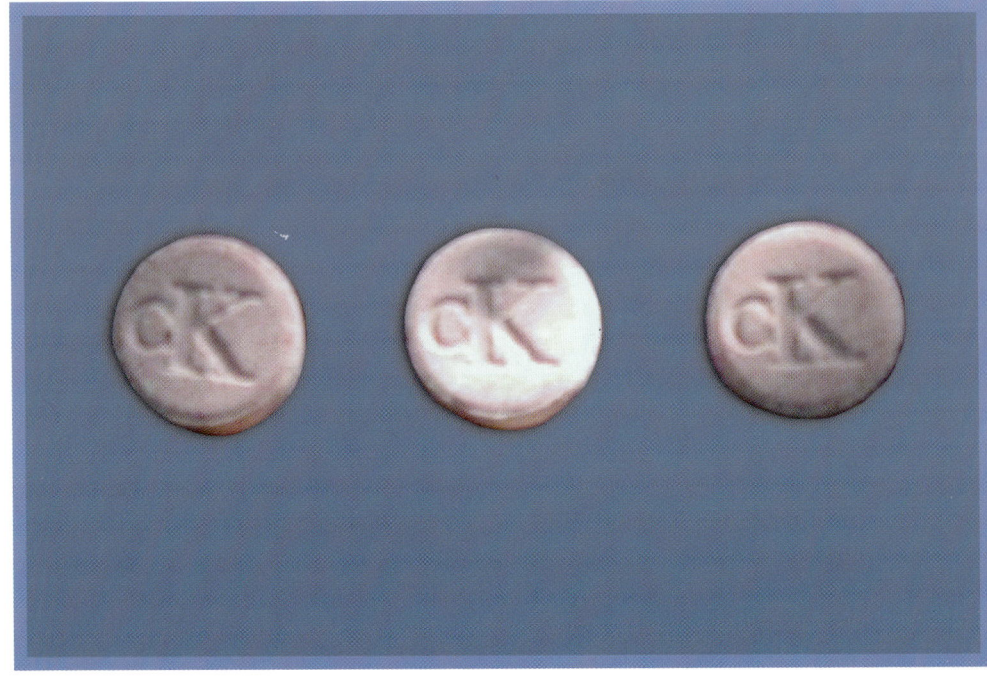

▲ *Ecstasy is usually taken in tablet form. Most ecstasy is smuggled into the United States from Europe.*

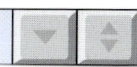

inhalants such as nitrous oxide (whippets). In recent years, use of party drugs has reached epidemic proportions. As of 2000, an estimated 6.4 million people had used ecstasy at least once in their lives. From 1998 to 2000, emergency-room admissions involving GHB nearly quadrupled. Emergency-room mentions of Rohypnol increased from 13 in 1994 to 624 in 1998.

Party drugs' side effects are downright frightening. They include vomiting, depression, paranoia, convulsions, and heart attacks. If users overdose on a party drug or mix a party drug with alcohol, they could wind up in a hospital, jail, or even as a dead body in the county morgue.

▶ Stories of Abuse

One young British woman described her experience with ecstasy in the *London Daily Telegraph*. At first, she believed ecstasy was a wonder drug. "However, after a while I realized that there were things going on in my head that weren't normal," she said.[5] She became uneasy, paranoid. She thought she was going mad. "Weird thoughts would terrify me," she said. "For a while I was convinced that I had a worm in my brain, or that my head was somehow just going to fly off into space. . . . I lay on my bed crying, for about five months, wanting to die."[6]

In suburban Detroit in 1999, three teenage girls hung out with four young men in an apartment on a Saturday night. One of the guys asked what the girls wanted to drink. Melanie asked for a mixed drink while Samantha requested a soda. Joshua poured the drinks for the girls—then spiked them with GHB. "We thought if we put a little into the drinks, maybe they'll liven up a bit," Joshua said later.[7]

Within minutes, Melanie began to vomit. Samantha passed out, but she vomited while unconscious. More upset by the mess the girls made, two of the guys went to a nearby store to buy cleaning supplies. After they got back, they heard Samantha gagging while Melanie was also very ill. Finally, at 4:30 A.M., they

> MyReportLinks.com Books

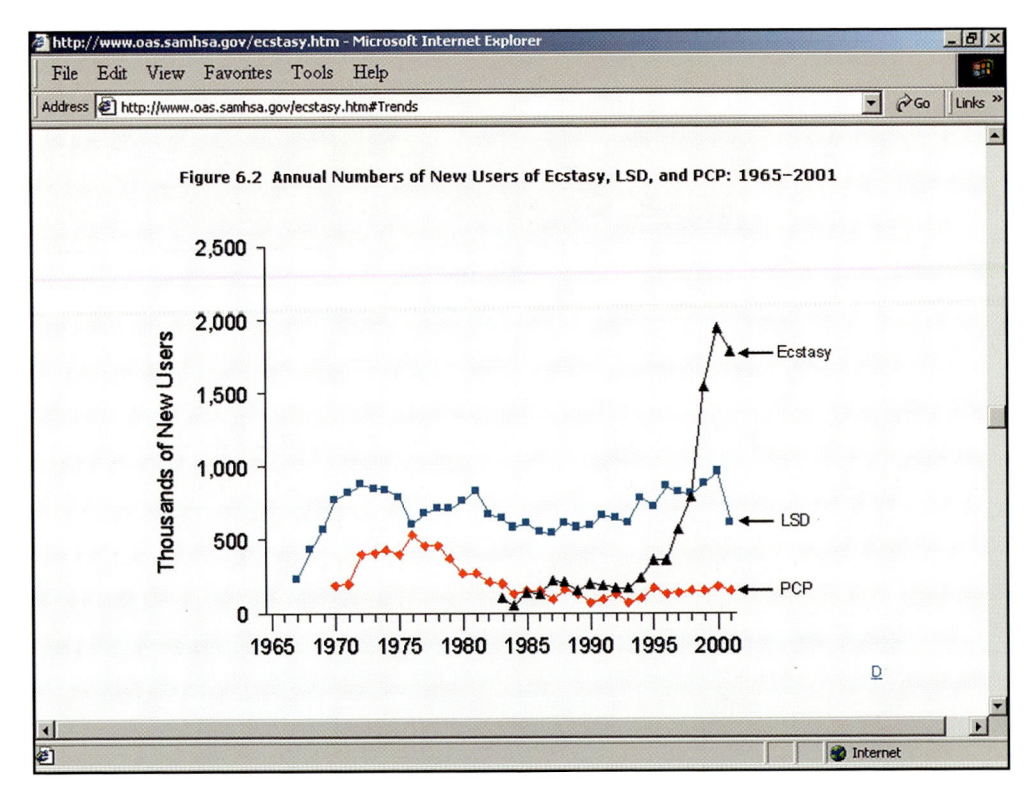

Figure 6.2 Annual Numbers of New Users of Ecstasy, LSD, and PCP: 1965–2001

▲ A graph comparing the number of new users of ecstasy, LSD, and PCP between 1965 and 2001. PCP is a hallucinogen commonly called angel dust.

drove Samantha and Melanie to the hospital. When they arrived, neither girl was breathing and neither had a heartbeat.

Melanie survived after lying in a coma for seventeen hours. Samantha did not make it. Joshua and the three other men were convicted of manslaughter. Three of the four young men were sentenced to up to fifteen years in Michigan State Prison.

Chapter 2

HISTORY OF PARTY DRUGS

During the late 1960s, the media reported that drug use was common among America's counterculture. Hippies and other young people smoked marijuana and abused other drugs, including amphetamines (known as speed), a stimulant. The federal government responded strongly, passing the Controlled Substances Act of 1970. This law banned the possession of numerous drugs, including amphetamines. This led to the tragic tale of designer drugs.

In 1976, a chemistry student in Maryland named Barry Kidston decided to synthesize his own drug—one similar in effect to amphetamines but not banned by the Controlled Substances Act. He created MPPP (1–methyl–4–phenyl–propionoxypiperidine), which he injected into his veins. One day, however, Kidston made a mistake and created MPTP (1–methyl–4–phenyl–1,2,3,6–tetrahydropyridine). Within three days of injecting it, he could no longer speak or move. Kidston's story was not an isolated case. In the 1980s, hundreds of people developed severe disabilities or died designing their own drugs.

Designer drugs were banned in the Controlled Substance Analog Act of 1986. Nevertheless, some designer drugs, such as ecstasy, steadily became more popular at raves, dance parties, and nightclubs beginning in the 1980s. From 1993 to 1998, ecstasy use quintupled in the United States. The drugs were so popular at these venues that some "designer drugs" became known as

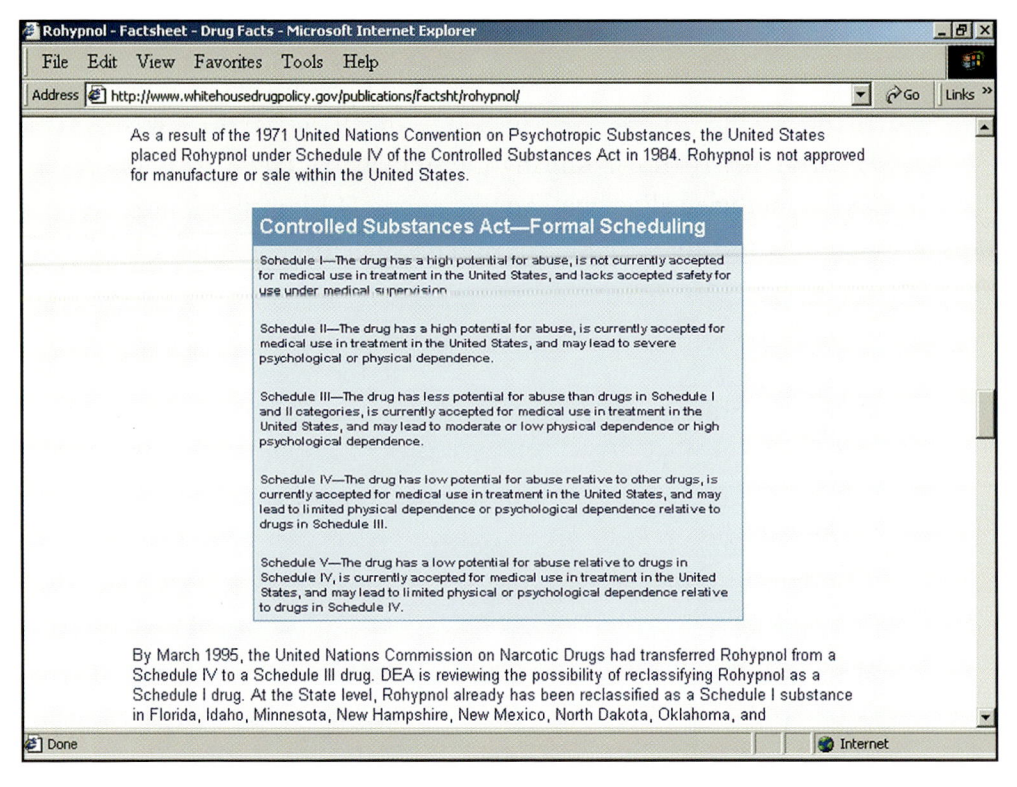

> Rohypnol - Factsheet - Drug Facts - Microsoft Internet Explorer
>
> http://www.whitehousedrugpolicy.gov/publications/factsht/rohypnol/
>
> As a result of the 1971 United Nations Convention on Psychotropic Substances, the United States placed Rohypnol under Schedule IV of the Controlled Substances Act in 1984. Rohypnol is not approved for manufacture or sale within the United States.
>
> **Controlled Substances Act—Formal Scheduling**
>
> Schedule I—The drug has a high potential for abuse, is not currently accepted for medical use in treatment in the United States, and lacks accepted safety for use under medical supervision.
>
> Schedule II—The drug has a high potential for abuse, is currently accepted for medical use in treatment in the United States, and may lead to severe psychological or physical dependence.
>
> Schedule III—The drug has less potential for abuse than drugs in Schedule I and II categories, is currently accepted for medical use in treatment in the United States, and may lead to moderate or low physical dependence or high psychological dependence.
>
> Schedule IV—The drug has low potential for abuse relative to other drugs, is currently accepted for medical use in treatment in the United States, and may lead to limited physical dependence or psychological dependence relative to drugs in Schedule III.
>
> Schedule V—The drug has a low potential for abuse relative to drugs in Schedule IV, is currently accepted for medical use in treatment in the United States, and may lead to limited physical or psychological dependence relative to drugs in Schedule IV.
>
> By March 1995, the United Nations Commission on Narcotic Drugs had transferred Rohypnol from a Schedule IV to a Schedule III drug. DEA is reviewing the possibility of reclassifying Rohypnol as a Schedule I drug. At the State level, Rohypnol already has been reclassified as a Schedule I substance in Florida, Idaho, Minnesota, New Hampshire, New Mexico, North Dakota, Oklahoma, and

▲ *The Controlled Substances Act places substances regulated under federal law into one of five schedules, or categories. On the federal level, MDMA is considered a Schedule I substance, defined by the federal government as having "a high potential for abuse, . . . not currently accepted for medical use."*

"party drugs" or "club drugs." With the emergence of the Internet, some dealers were able to sell party drugs online.

The term "predatory drugs" emerged in the mid-1990s. Across the United States, there were dozens of cases of women waking up naked in strange places with no memory of what had happened to them. Police discovered that men had laced the women's drinks with GHB, then raped them after their bodies fell limp. Congress reacted quickly, passing the Drug-Induced Rape Prevention and Punishment Act of 1996. Nevertheless, 15 to 20 percent of all rapes committed in the early 2000s were drug induced.

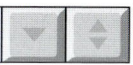

The Rise of Ecstasy

Though it would not be called ecstasy for decades, the drug MDMA was first synthesized in 1912. In 1914, MDMA was patented by the Merck Company in Germany. MDMA is short for 3, 4–methylenedioxymethamphetamine. Originally, it was thought that the drug would help stop patients from bleeding too much. In the 1950s, the United States Army tested to see whether MDMA could be used to get people to tell the truth. However, people found little use for MDMA until the 1960s, when a California chemist named Alexander Shulgin got his hands on it. In 1967, Shulgin made his own batch of the drug, consumed it, and wrote, "[T]here is nothing but pure euphoria. I have never felt so great or believed this to be possible."[1]

Shulgin spread the word about MDMA to his psychologist friends. Also in 1967, the chemically related MDA (3, 4–methylenedioxyamphetamine) became a popular drug with California youth.[2] MDA, but not MDMA, was made illegal in 1970.

MDMA was prescribed by some psychiatrists in the 1970s and early 1980s. These doctors thought MDMA might help people who lacked confidence to overcome their problems. Few recreational drug users took MDMA until 1984. That year, a dealer in Texas heavily advertised the drug and sold it through a toll-free number. Soon the drug became popular, earning the name "ecstasy." MDMA enhanced users' sights and sounds, making it a big hit at parties, dance clubs, and raves. Like alcohol, it was a social drug. Its "love" effect gave partiers a feeling of togetherness.

In the meantime, doctors discovered the horrible side effects of ecstasy. In July 1985, the U.S. Drug Enforcement Administration (DEA) used its emergency scheduling power to make MDMA illegal. Nevertheless, the drug flourished underground. Worldwide ecstasy abuse jumped 70 percent from 1995 to 2001.

Ecstasy, according to the DEA, ". . . is by far the most popular of the party drugs."[3] But it is not the only one. Ketamine first emerged in the 1960s as an anesthetic and recreational drug.

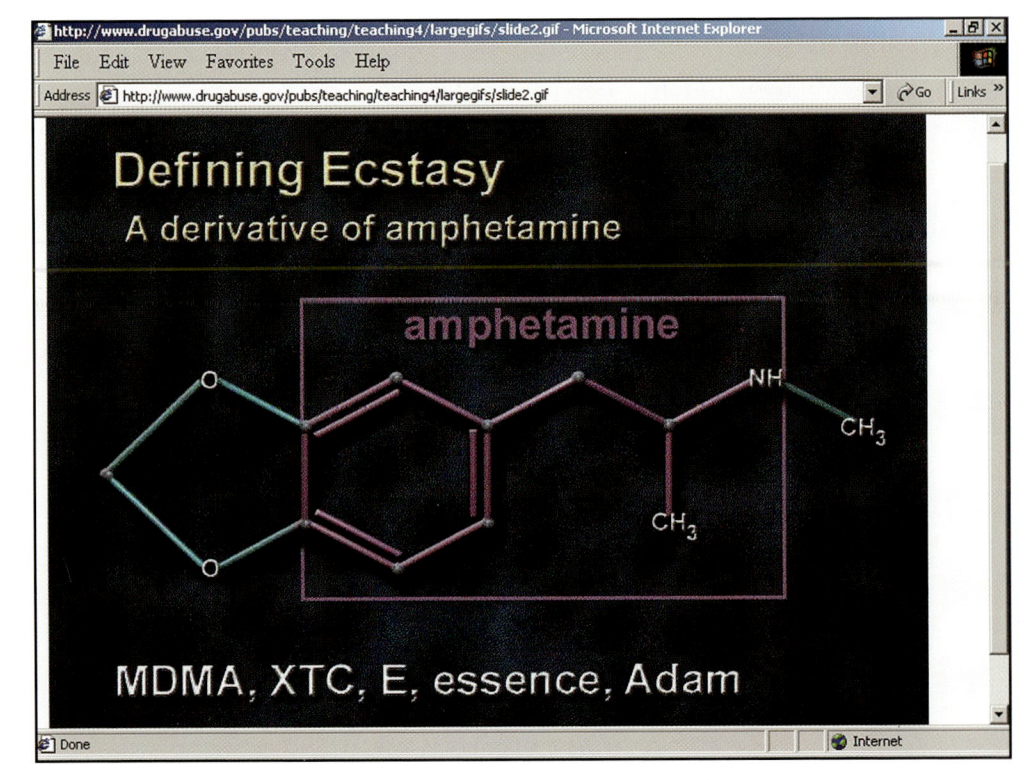

▲ MDMA, a derivative of amphetamine, is similar in structure to methamphetamine. MDMA is made in a laboratory, and depending upon who makes the drug, it can vary in purity. In the past, labs have included caffeine, ephedrine, and ketamine in making MDMA tablets.

Abuse of ketamine has risen in recent years. LSD, a hallucinogen glamorized in the 1960s, became trendy once again toward the end of the twentieth century.

▶ Emergence of Predatory Drugs

GHB and Rohypnol are the two most common predatory drugs. They have one thing in common: They put people to sleep. Sadly, sometimes the people do not wake up.

GHB was first synthesized in the 1960s for use as a pain reliever. Eventually, bodybuilders purchased the substance in health food stores, claiming that it aided in reducing fat and developing muscles. These claims were never proven. However, GHB was proven to depress breathing and nervous system functions, causing some people to lose consciousness. After two men overdosed on GHB and died in 1990, the Food and Drug Administration banned over-the-counter sales of the drug.

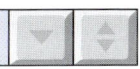

Throughout the 1990s, hundreds of people became ill on GHB, and many died. Moreover, some men discovered that they could use GHB as an aid to rape women. GHB combined with alcohol would cause a woman to be "knocked out" for hours, and she would awake with no memory of the night before. In 2000, President Bill Clinton signed the Hillory J. Farias and Samantha Reid Date-Rape Drug Prohibition Act. This act was named after two young women who had died after unknowingly taking GHB that had been slipped in their sodas. This law made GHB a Schedule 1 drug throughout the United States, making it a felony to even possess GHB.

In the late 1990s, Rohypnol became the date-rape drug of choice. Sexual predators liked the effect of the drug. It was ten

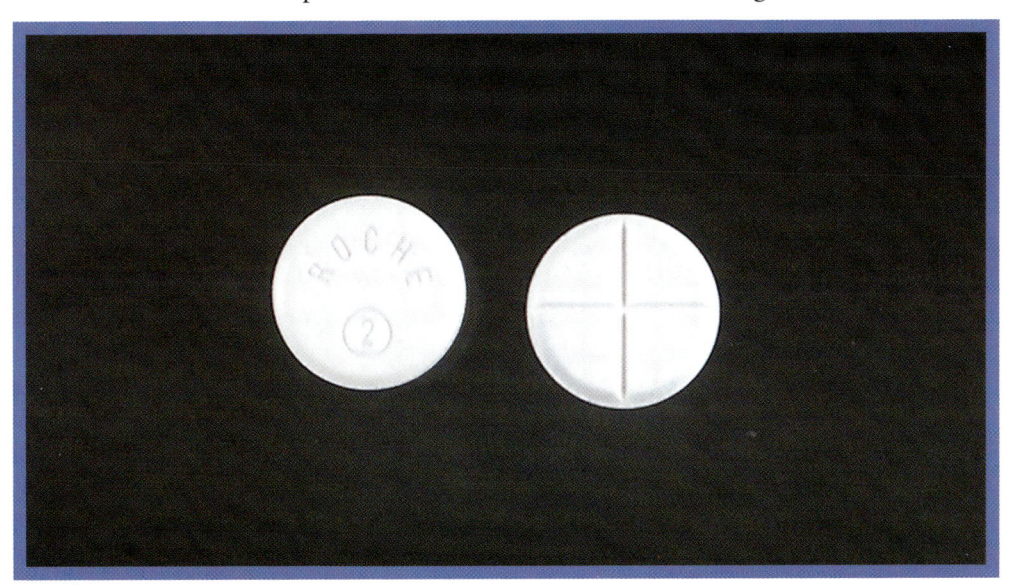

▲ *Rohypnol became a well-known drug in the late 1990s. In most cases, men would slip a Rohypnol tablet into a woman's drink without her knowing it. The effects of the drug would usually make her unable to resist a rape.*

STREET NAMES FOR PARTY AND PREDATORY DRUGS

DRUG	STREET NAMES
MDMA	Adam, B-bombs, Beans, Clarity, Cristal, Decadence, Dex, Disco biscuit, Ecstasy, E, Essence, Eve, Go, Hug drug, Iboga, Love drug, Morning shot, Pollutants, Scooby Snacks, Speed for lovers, Sweeties, Wheels, X, XTC
GHB	Cherry Meth, Fantasy, GBH, Georgia home boy, Great hormones at bedtime, Grievous bodily harm, Liquid E, Liquid Ecstasy, Liquid X, Organic quaalude, Salty water, Scoop, Sleep-500, Soap, Somatomaz, Vita G
Rohypnol	Circles, Forget me drug, Forget me pill, Getting roached, La Rocha, Lunch money drug, Mexican valium, Pingus, R-2, Reynolds, Rib, Roach-2, Roapies, Robutol, Roofies, Rope, Rophies, Row-shay, Ruffles, Wolfies
Ketamine	Cat Valium, Green, Jet, K, Special K, Super acid
Methamphetamine	Bikers coffee, Chalk, Chicken Feed, Crank, Crystal Meth, Glass, Go-Fast, Ice, Methlies Quick, Poor Man's Cocaine, Shabu, Speed, Stove Top, Trash, Yellow Bam
Amyl Nitrate	Ames, Amies, Amys, Bolt, Bullet, Pearls, Poppers
LSD	Acid, Blotter, Dots, Mellow Yellow, Window Pane

*Source: Office of National Drug Control Policy

times stronger than Valium and caused victims to sleep eight to twelve hours.

Though these and other date-rape drugs are illegal in the United States, they still are sometimes sold on the Internet. The FBI recently shut down a site that provided a "Date Rape Kit." For $49.95, the kit included ingredients to make GHB and an instructional video on how to obtain a female victim.[4] The United States government has stepped up efforts to crack down on predatory drugs and educate the nation on their effects.

Chapter 3

EFFECTS OF PARTY DRUGS

"The great lie about ecstasy," said John Walters of the Office of National Drug Control Policy, "is that it is safe, it's fun, it's harmless, and it's fashionable."[1] The parents of Brandy French would agree. Their daughter died at age sixteen after taking just one ecstasy tablet.

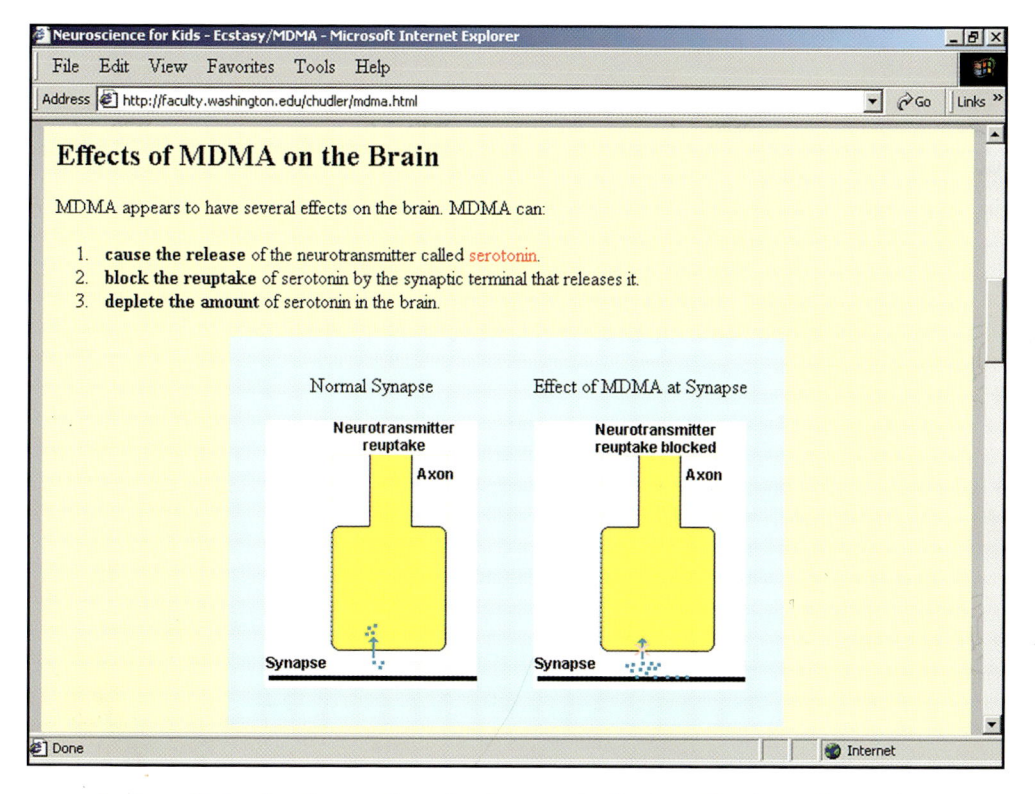

Effects of MDMA on the Brain

MDMA appears to have several effects on the brain. MDMA can:

1. **cause the release** of the neurotransmitter called serotonin.
2. **block the reuptake** of serotonin by the synaptic terminal that releases it.
3. **deplete the amount** of serotonin in the brain.

Normal Synapse — Neurotransmitter reuptake — Axon — Synapse

Effect of MDMA at Synapse — Neurotransmitter reuptake blocked — Axon — Synapse

▲ An effect of using ecstasy is damage to brain cells that release the neurotransmitter serotonin. This can hinder a person's ability to remember and learn.

The Truth About Ecstasy

MDMA is related to MDA, which is derived from the oils of sassafras, saffron, nutmeg, and crocus. Chemists can restructure the molecules of MDA to create numerous drugs, but users prefer the effects of MDMA the best.

Besides the name ecstasy, MDMA's street terms include XTC, Adam, hug, beans, and love drug. Some just call it E. Other substances are sometimes mixed into ecstasy, such as caffeine, amphetamine, and/or baking soda. Some contaminants are extremely toxic, such as PMA (paramethoxyamphetamine or 4–methoxyamphetamine).

Ecstasy is both a stimulant and a hallucinogen. After taking this drug, users feel its effects in about a half hour. Initially, they feel energetic, wide awake, and not hungry. Their body temperature, heart rate, and blood pressure rise. They become sweaty and thirsty, and they might feel anxious and tingly.

These reactions diminish and give way to euphoric feelings: serenity, happiness, a love for other people. These effects last for hours. Users like to take ecstasy with other people because of the "love" aspect of the drug. They also prefer it at parties and dance clubs since the drug enhances sights and sounds.

Ecstasy users always risk a "bad trip." Instead of pleasure, they might feel anxious and panicked. That is among the least of ecstasy's side effects. MDMA can lead to double vision, nausea, hallucinations, vomiting, muscle cramping, and tremors. It often causes involuntary teeth clenching (which is why some ecstasy users chew on pacifiers). Ecstasy can cause dehydration, which can lead to heat stroke, kidney failure, and respiratory collapse.

Ecstasy increases a person's heart rate and blood pressure, which is dangerous for those with circulatory or heart disease. It can also damage the liver as well as parts of the brain critical to thought and memory. Ecstasy users have suffered seizures, strokes, and heart attacks. Anthony Tarantino of Las Vegas suffered brain and eye damage. "My eyesight is just totally shot,

▶ Effects of Party Drugs

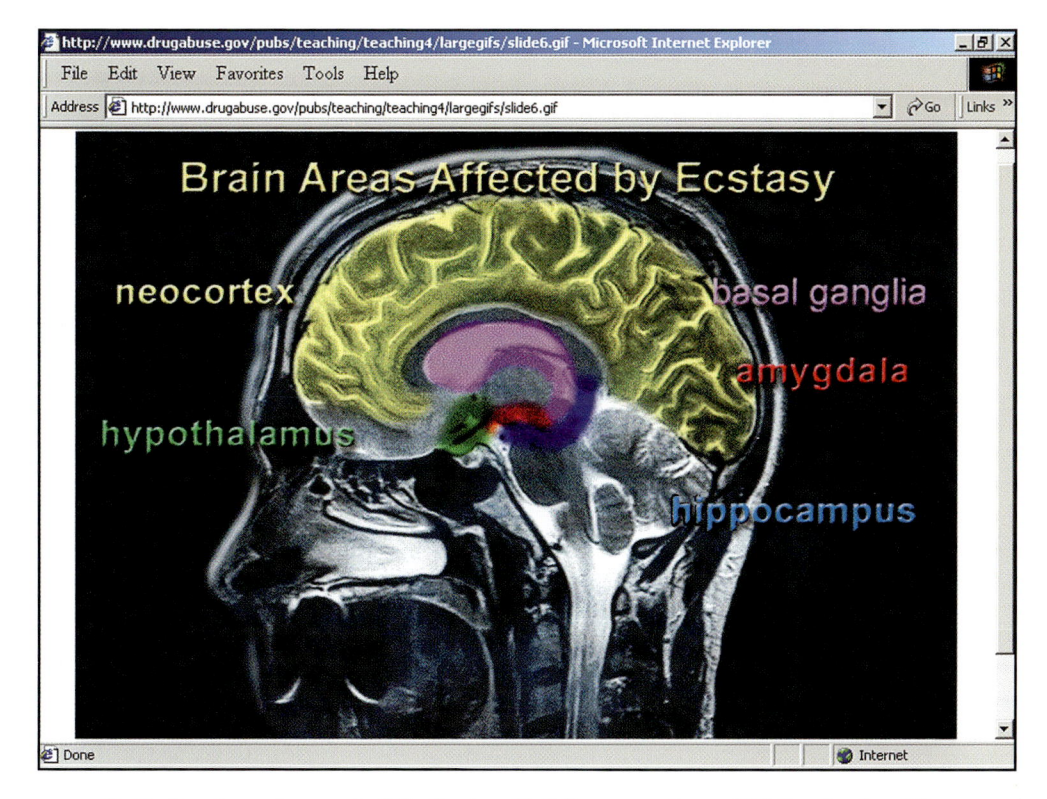

▲ Ecstasy impacts a part of the brain called the neocortex, which has to do with your memory and perception. The drug also affects a person's amygdala, hippocampus, basal ganglia, and hypothalamus, the sections of the brain that alter your emotions and moods.

damaged," he said. "I see . . . light and colors and stuff that aren't even there."[2]

The more a person takes ecstasy, the greater the risks. Repeated usage of the drug disrupts the body's serotonin levels. Proper serotonin is needed to regulate mood, aggression, sleep, and sensitivity to pain. Too much ecstasy can lead to depression, sleep problems, severe anxiety, and paranoia. These effects can last for weeks to months after taking MDMA.

Those who take ecstasy are clearly risking their lives. In England and Wales in 2001 and 2002, seventy-two people died because of ecstasy. Of those, about 17 percent had not mixed MDMA with alcohol or any other drug.

▶ Ketamine's Not-So-Special Effects

Ketamine, short for ketamine hydrochloride, is a muscle relaxer. Legal with a prescription, it is used by doctors, veterinarians, and psychiatrists for various purposes. Mostly, though, ketamine is abused by thrill-seekers at clubs, raves, and parties. They refer to it as special K, vitamin K, kit kat, cat valium, and K.

As a liquid, ketamine can be injected into muscles or veins. It can also be evaporated into powder, then sniffed or smoked. Whatever the form, the drug is extremely powerful. Ketamine relieves tension and intensifies sounds and colors, but the drug comes with plenty of baggage. Users tend to hallucinate and have out-of-body experiences. This is called "dropping in the k-hole" or a black hole. Their breathing slows, and their speech slurs. They may feel numb, lose coordination, feel invincible, and become violent. This combination makes them dangerous to themselves and others.

Large doses of ketamine can cause vomiting, convulsions, and starvation of oxygen to the brain. Long-term use could lead to psychological and/or physical addiction. Flashbacks can occur a year after usage. Those who overdose on ketamine can fall into a coma. A single gram can kill a healthy adult.

▶ "Tripping" on LSD

Popular in the 1960s, LSD has resurfaced as a party drug in recent years. On the street, it is known as acid, blotter, ghost, electric Kool-Aid, and more than a hundred other names. The chemical name for LSD is lysergic acid diethylamide.

LSD, which comes in tablet and capsule form, does not have any significant medical benefits. It is a hallucinogen used by recreational drug users. Proponents of LSD say the drug helps people to free their minds. However, the effects of "tripping" on

▶ Effects of Party Drugs

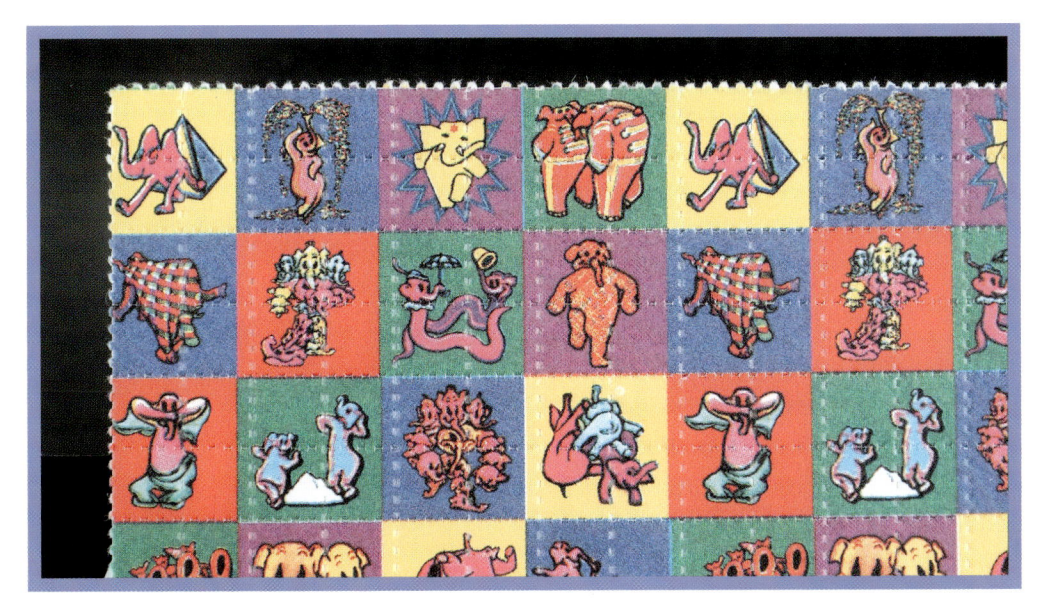

▲ LSD is usually distributed on a sheet that looks a little like a sheet of postage stamps. Each stamp is called a "tab." People that abuse LSD can have disorienting flashbacks later in life.

LSD are wildly unpredictable. Using the drug can impair one's perception of depth, time, movements, and size and shape of objects. According to Drugs.com, "Sensations may seem to 'cross over,' giving the feeling of hearing colors and seeing sounds."[3]

LSD users can experience great anxiety, terrifying thoughts, and fear of insanity. These feelings may last for hours. The drug raises one's body temperature and heart rate. It can cause sleeplessness, nausea, dizziness, and tremors. Long-term use can lead to severe depression and even schizophrenia. Doctors will tell you that this drug is not worth the trip.

▶ **Predators' Favorite Drugs**

Predatory drugs are most commonly used by men to sedate and rape women. Some people consider rape a sexual fantasy, but in reality it is an extremely serious crime. In the United States, rape is a Class B felony, punishable by up to twenty-five years in prison.

Moreover, predatory drugs are highly dangerous themselves. They can lead to blackouts, seizures, and even death. The most commonly used predatory drugs are GHB and Rohypnol.

GHB is short for gamma hydroxybutyrate. Drug dealers refer to this illegal drug as liquid X, liquid E, salty water, and more than eighty other names. GHB is an odorless, colorless liquid. It is not chemically related to ecstasy, but some of the effects are the same. A rapist will try to pour it into his date's drink when she is not looking.

If given a certain dosage of GHB, a person initially will feel euphoric and uninhibited—as well as very groggy. It is in this stage that a sexual predator takes advantage of his victim. The rapist also likes GHB's amnesia effect. Many of those who awake from a GHB-induced sleep cannot remember what happened the night before.

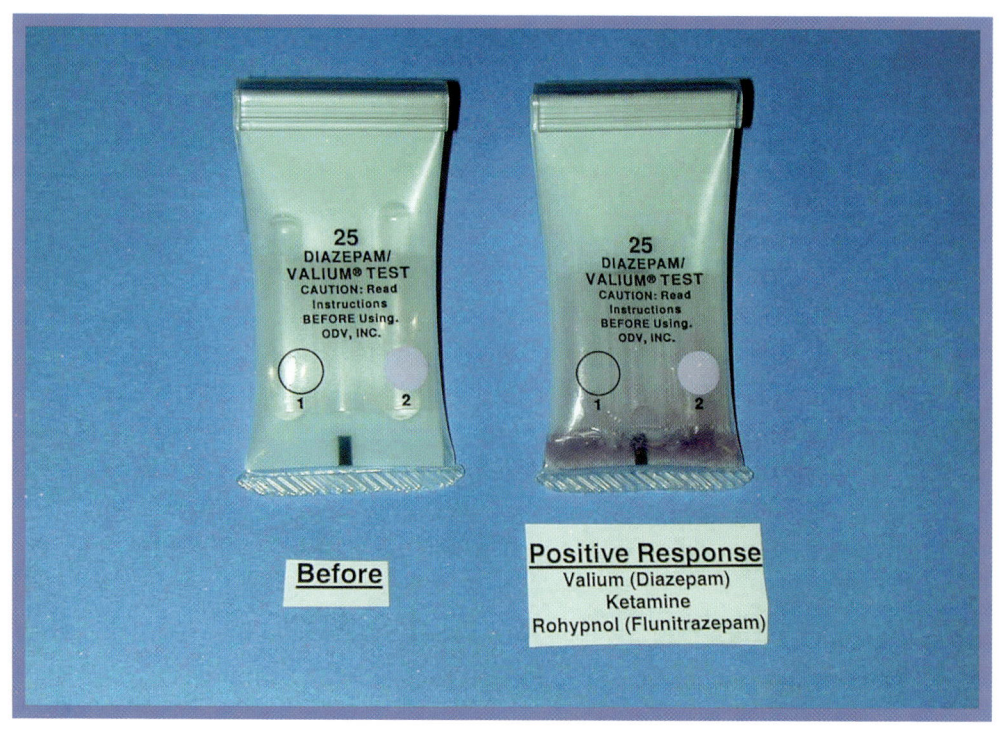

▲ This kit is used by law enforcement to test whether ketamine or Rohypnol has been slipped into a drink. It also tests for Valium, a type of tranquilizer.

What is especially frightening is that a slight overdose of GHB can have devastating effects on the body. The victim may suffer a seizure, lose consciousness, or possibly fall into a coma. Her pulse might slow to only a few heartbeats per minute. GHB often induces vomiting, even if the user is unconscious. Many of those who die from GHB suffocate on their own vomit.

GHB's effects are wildly unpredictable, especially since a batch could have been cooked up in an amateur's laboratory and the buyer does not know what is in it. "The dose that might make a 150-pound girl high could kill a 300-pound man," says former narcotics detective Trinka Porrata. "And the dose that made you high yesterday might kill you today."[4]

GHB is more than just a date-rape drug. Some partiers take a teaspoon of GHB for a quick, strong "buzz." Some people take GHB as a sleep aid, which most doctors say is foolish. Many bodybuilders and athletes have tried it as a means to build muscle. Since they take it regularly, they are the most likely to become addicted to the drug.

GHB is illegal, so immoral chemists have developed "chemical cousins" of GHB. The most common are GBL, BD, and GHV. Though these substances are sold at gyms and on the Internet, they are similar to GHB and extremely dangerous. Wrote one woman about GBL, "My daughter died from a recommended, standard dose as stated on the bottle. No overdose. No other chemicals in her body. Not even aspirin."[5] As of 2002, the DEA had documented seventy-two deaths relating to GHB and its derivatives.

Rohypnol is another date-rape drug. Known by chemists as flunitrazepam, it is referred to in clubs as roofies, rophies, rope, and the forget pill. Rohypnol tablets are illegal in the United States but legal in many countries, including Mexico. Rohypnol's effects are similar to those of alcohol. In fact, many users grind roofie tablets into a beer to get "wasted" cheaply and quickly.

Since Rohypnol is a sedative, some men use it to take advantage of women.

Just minutes after ingesting Rohypnol, the victim may feel dizzy, disoriented, and nauseous. She might feel restless and experience hallucinations. The victim likely will lose inhibition, and her arms will go limp. In this stage, she is unable to fend off the sexual advances of her date. Typically, the victim passes out, sleeping for six to ten hours. Since the drug decreases oxygen to the brain, she could awake with amnesia—remembering little or nothing from the night before. Sometimes, victims never wake up.

▶ Other Party Drugs

Ecstasy, ketamine, LSD, GHB, and Rohypnol are the most popular party drugs. Others, though, creep into clubs, dance halls,

▲ Methamphetamine is a very dangerous party drug. The form of methamphetamine shown here is called ice because it looks like ice crystals. Also shown is a pipe used to smoke this drug.

parties, and schools. Methamphetamine and amyl nitrate are two troublesome drugs.

Methamphetamine is an illegal, highly dangerous stimulant. Users refer to it as meth or speed. Available in all forms, it can be swallowed, injected, sniffed, or smoked. Meth users experience a euphoria, but at a heavy price. The long list of side effects includes confusion, tremors, convulsions, paranoia, strokes, cardiovascular collapse, and death. Methamphetamine is highly addictive. The more addicts take it, the more damage they are causing to their body.

Amyl nitrate is known as poppers. Users inhale amyl nitrate's fishy-smelling vapors, which lowers their blood pressure and increases their pulse rate. Users feel relaxed and tranquil, but the side effects are severe. Users may experience dizziness, respiratory problems, and blackouts. Those who overdose may die.

▶ Killer Cocktails

If people are selling ecstasy tablets at a party, it is likely that other drugs are floating around, too. Alcohol, cocaine, amphetamines, and other drugs may be available. Once a partier is high on one of these drugs, she might accept when offered another. Abusing a variety of drugs during the same evening is referred to as "cafeteria-style" drug use. Those who do it are risking their lives.

"Many people now combine Ecstasy with alcohol at the beginning of the evening to get a greater high," says Dr. Fabrizio Schifano of St. George's Hospital Medical School in London. "[They] then use drugs like cocaine or amphetamines to prolong the effect, before taking opiates or high doses of alcohol to calm themselves down at the end of the evening." He adds that "it's a potentially lethal cocktail."[6]

Often, the only way a sexual predator can slip his date GHB or Rohypnol is to drop it into her alcoholic drink. These drugs are already potent enough. Alcohol greatly increases their effects, putting the victim's life at risk.

Chapter 4

How Party Drugs Are Made and Sold

The production of party and predatory drugs varies greatly depending on the drug. Some types are manufactured legally in the United States, though many are not. Ecstasy, the most abused party drug, is illegal in every country in the world due to the United Nations Commission on Narcotic Drugs.

▶ Manufacturing Party Drugs

Most of the world's ecstasy is produced illegally in secret laboratories in the Netherlands. This European country is the center of the international chemical industry. This makes it easier for the

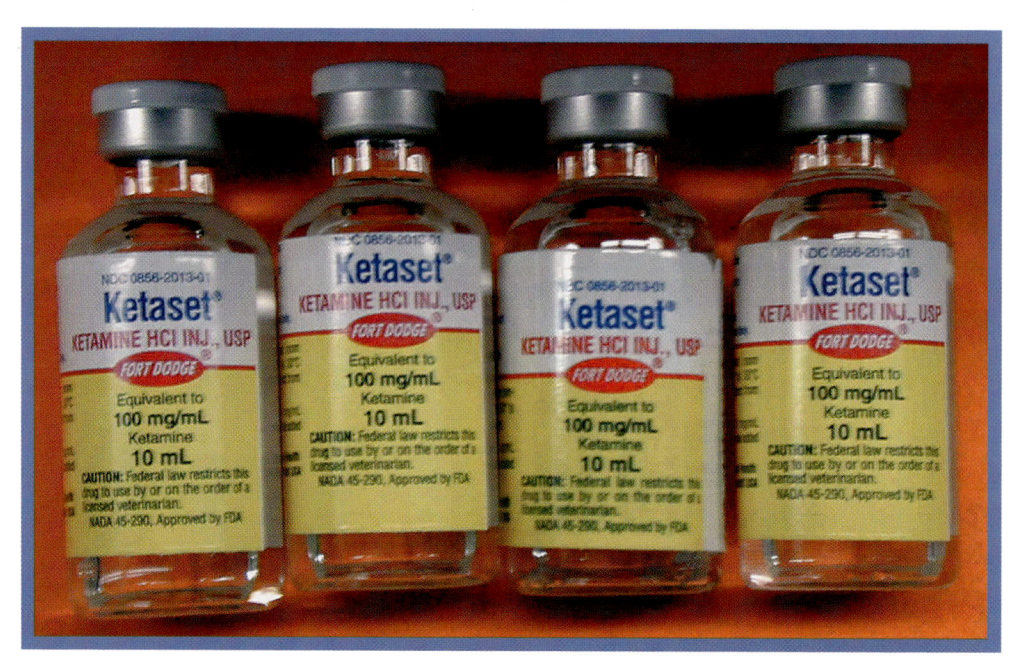

▲ *Ketamine is a strong painkiller used by doctors to treat humans, but more often by veterinarians to calm animals while they are being treated.*

criminals to get the ingredients to make ecstasy. The drug is also produced in Belgium, Poland, Myanmar, Thailand, and the Middle East—as well as in the United States.

Most LSD laboratories in the United States have been found in northern California. This illegal drug is difficult to make, and only a few chemists produce it on a regular basis. Ketamine is manufactured legally in the United States because it is a useful painkiller for humans and animals. The DEA has found no evidence that ketamine is produced in secret laboratories—largely because it is extremely difficult to make.

Rohypnol is not legally manufactured or sold in the United States. Yet in some countries, including Mexico, it is legally produced and prescribed as a sleep aid. GHB is manufactured legally in some foreign countries and illegally in the United States. Amateur chemists can make GHB if they have GBL. GBL is legal in some states and widely available on the Internet. What is scary is that much of the amateur-made GHB contains too high of a dose of GBL. Thus, says Dr. Westley Clark, those who take a hit (dose) of GHB are taking a big chance with their lives.[1]

Selling Party Drugs

Authorities believe that Israeli organized crime syndicates smuggle large amounts of ecstasy from Europe to the United States. They do so by express mail, via couriers on commercial airline flights, and through airfreight shipments. Actually, criminals in many countries now traffic ecstasy. Much of it arrives in Canada and Mexico, where it is smuggled over the United States border.

Drug dealers in the United States sell ecstasy at parties, at clubs, on school grounds, and on the Internet. Much of it is sold at raves. These huge dance parties, once held in warehouses, are now being held in concert halls and underground parking lots. Raves feature electronic music, light shows, and plenty of drugs. Partiers (most aged fifteen to twenty-five) hear about local raves via the Internet or word of mouth.

Peddlers at raves sell ecstasy trinkets, including glow sticks and pacifiers. Ecstasy users tend to involuntarily grind their teeth, so they need pacifiers to stop them from getting damaged. Ecstasy tablets cost about twenty to thirty dollars. They often feature a distinctive brand logo, such as a smiley face, butterfly, or four-leaf clover. Those who take E tend to carry bottled water, since the drug causes dehydration.

In the United States and Mexico, criminals often steal ketamine from pharmacies and veterinary clinics. Veterinarians use it to help relax animals. Though it comes in a liquid form, dealers fry it into a powder. Eventually, a 100- or 200-milligram dose is sold on the street or at raves for about twenty dollars. Increasingly in recent years, dealers have mixed other powdery drugs in with ketamine, including cocaine and amphetamines. Some partiers prefer LSD because it is cheaper. An average hit costs about five dollars.

Technically, Rohypnol is available in Mexico only through a prescription. Yet corruption is common, and dealers have found

▲ Ecstasy tablets usually feature a brand stamp on their center. The tablets shown here are stamped with the butterfly brand. Some brands may have effects that are slightly different from others.

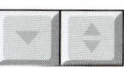

ways to get the drug and then smuggle it into the United States. Colombian drug dealers are also involved in obtaining Rohypnol and trafficking it to the United States. GHB takes different routes to the States. Much arrives via mail services from Europe, while a large amount is smuggled in vehicles from Canada. GHB is sold at raves and dance clubs. Dealers also peddle it on the Internet as a cleaning product or a nail polish remover.

How Men Use Date-Rape Drugs

If a man intends to rape a woman using a predatory drug, he will usually slip the drug into her drink. Because GHB and Rohypnol are colorless and odorless, this is pretty easy to do. The date rapist usually hides the drug in a water, eye drop, or mouthwash bottle. When the woman is not looking, he pours the drug into her drink. Charly Cutler, president of Guardian Angel GHB Test Kits, explains what happens next:

"First, women get lightheaded and sway back and forth. Then there is a 15-minute time period for the man to go up, make nice to the girl, and then take her out before anyone notices. It may even look like flirting. The guy suggests they go outside for a breath of air, and before you know it, he's taking the girl to his car so he can take her somewhere else and violate her."[2]

For the rapist, it seems like a surefire plan. Yet so many things could go wrong for him. The woman may realize she is being drugged and report the man. If she does pass out, she could require emergency care. The next morning, she or a witness may remember the man and recall what he did. If arrested, he faces serious consequences.

Legal Consequences

To certain young people, party drugs may seem like harmless fun. Doctors, ER workers, and victims of the drugs know better. These drugs are dangerous and illegal, and law enforcement officials are cracking down.

> MyReportLinks.com Books

> DEA Resources, For Law Enforcement Officers, Intelligence Reports, Rohypnol - Microsoft Internet Explorer
>
> File   Edit   View   Favorites   Tools   Help
>
> Address http://www.usdoj.gov/dea/pubs/rohypnol/rohypnol.htm
>
> urinalysis testing.
>
> Flunitrazepam is sold under the trade name Rohypnol, from which the street name "Rophy" is derived. In South Florida, street names include "circles," "Mexican valium," "rib," "roach-2," "roofies," "roopies," "rope," "ropies," and "ruffies." Being under the influence of the drug is referred to as being "roached out." In Texas, flunitrazepam is called "R-2," or "roaches."
>
> Rohypnol tablets are white and are single- or cross-scored on one side with "ROCHE" and "1" or "2" encircled on the other.
>
> **Scheduling**
>
> In 1983, flunitrazepam was placed into Schedule IV of the 1971 United Nations Convention on Psychotropic Substances. To comply with the convention, the United States placed flunitrazepam in Schedule IV of the Controlled Substances Act of 1970 (CSA), despite little evidence of its abuse. In March 1995, flunitrazepam was moved to Schedule III by the World Health Organization, requiring more thorough record keeping on its licit distribution—the first benzodiazepine to require more rigid controls. However, due to recent increases in seizures and abuse of this drug, DEA currently is reviewing the possibility of placing flunitrazepam into Schedule I of the CSA. A Schedule I drug is considered to have a high potential for abuse, to have no currently accepted medical use in treatment, and to lack accepted levels of safety for use under medical supervision.
>
> **Outlook**
>
> The distribution and abuse of flunitrazepam, in all likelihood, will continue to increase within certain segments of society in the United States, particularly among abusers of other illicit drugs and high school students who mistakenly believe that the drug is harmless. Of greatest concern to drug law
>
> Done   Internet

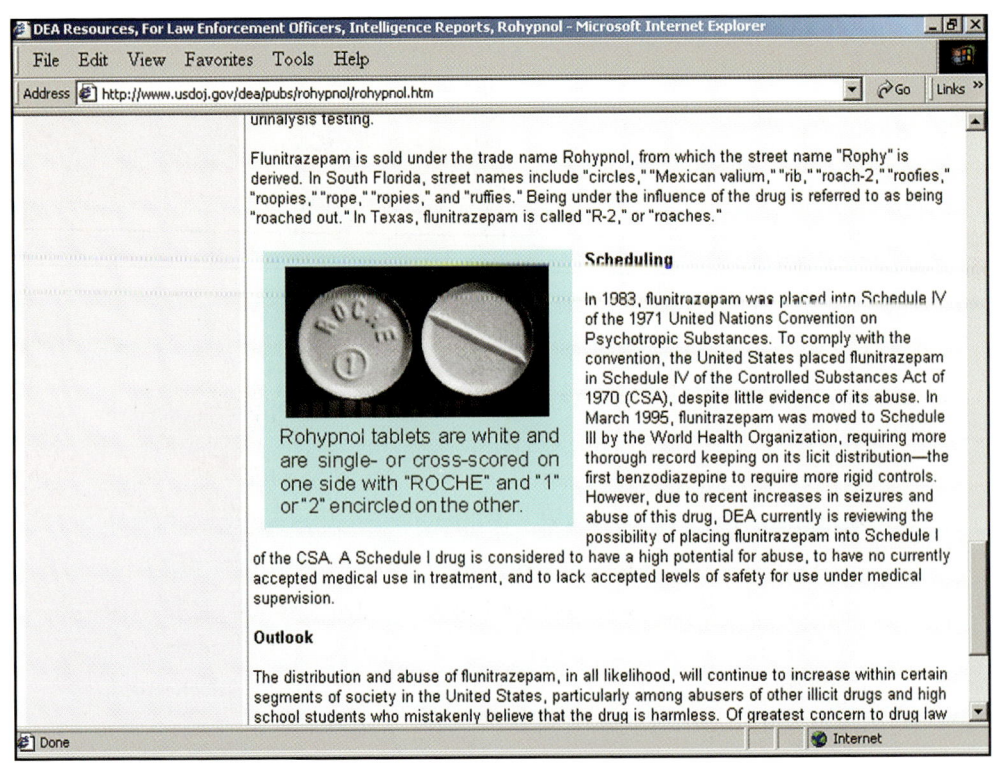

▲ *Flunitrazepam, commonly referred to as Rohypnol or roofies, comes in the form of a white tablet. It is manufactured by Hoffman-La Roche, Inc., a pharmaceutical company.*

In September 2002, federal officials broke an Internet ring of date-rape drug traffickers. They arrested 115 people in 84 cities. Said U.S. Attorney General John Ashcroft, "[T]he Internet is no longer a safe haven where drug dealers can hide. Our campuses, our neighborhoods and our communities are safer places for young women today because cyberspace just got more dangerous for drug traffickers."[3]

In the first half of 2000, U.S. Customs confiscated 5.4 million hits of ecstasy. In 2000 and 2001, the DEA seized a dozen illegal GHB laboratories. It is not just the dealers who are in trouble. All across the country, undercover officers are hiding out

How Party Drugs Are Made and Sold

Stopping drug dealers and buyers is one of the major aims of law enforcement officials. United States federal law states that a first-time offender could face up to one year in jail for simply possessing a small amount of ecstasy.

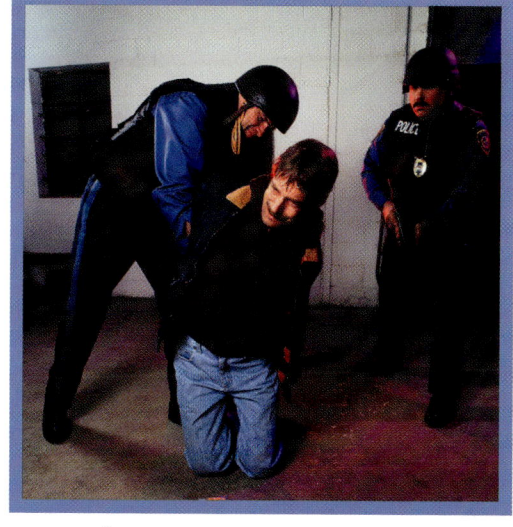

in clubs and at raves. People who buy or sell a single ecstasy pill could wind up in an officer's handcuffs and tossed into jail.

According to federal law, a person faces up to a year in prison for first-offense possession of ecstasy, LSD, ketamine, or GHB. Possession of Rohypnol carries a sentence of up to three years. A man who drugs a woman with Rohypnol (or certain other predatory drugs) with intent to commit rape faces up to twenty years in state prison. A person could also be sentenced to twenty years for trafficking a party drug or predatory drug.

Because of new technology, date rapists are being caught before they even leave the barstool. Foreign companies are manufacturing Rohypnol tablets that turn blue in a drink. Some would-be rapists are not aware of this until the drink changes colors before their eyes. Also, well prepared women are packing date-rape drug test strips in their purses. If the woman splashes a couple drops of her drink on a test strip and it turns blue, the drink contains a predatory drug. The would-be rapist is busted.

HOMESTEAD H.S. MEDIA CENTER
4310 HOMESTEAD ROAD
FORT WAYNE, IN 46814

Chapter 5

Avoiding Party Drugs, Getting Help

All across the nation, young people are lured by the "love drug" and other party drugs. They come mostly from the middle and upper-middle classes. Some are bored and looking for a thrill. Some are lonely, depressed, or looking to rebel. Others are self-conscious and inhibited, looking to free themselves. They think ecstasy or another party drug is the answer. Unfortunately, they are sadly misinformed. There is more than just the severe physical, psychological, and legal consequences of using party drugs. Drug users can also be expelled from sports teams, social clubs, and even school. The lesson to learn is unmistakable: Party drugs ruin lives.

▶ Warning Signs

Any party drug could cause a person to have a bad, sometimes life-threatening, reaction. A common and serious problem among ecstasy users is dehydration. If an ecstasy user has been dancing, but not sweating, and is suffering from cramps, dizziness, and/or nausea, he or she should be splashed with water and taken to the hospital. Any drug user who is having difficulty coping with his or her symptoms should be driven to the nearest emergency room by car or ambulance.

A drug user who passes out and cannot be easily awoken definitely needs emergency care. Do not hope that the person will "just sleep it off." Many young people die because their friends do not want to be linked to someone who overdosed. Such "friends" often wind up in prison for participating in murder or manslaughter.

Avoiding Party Drugs, Getting Help

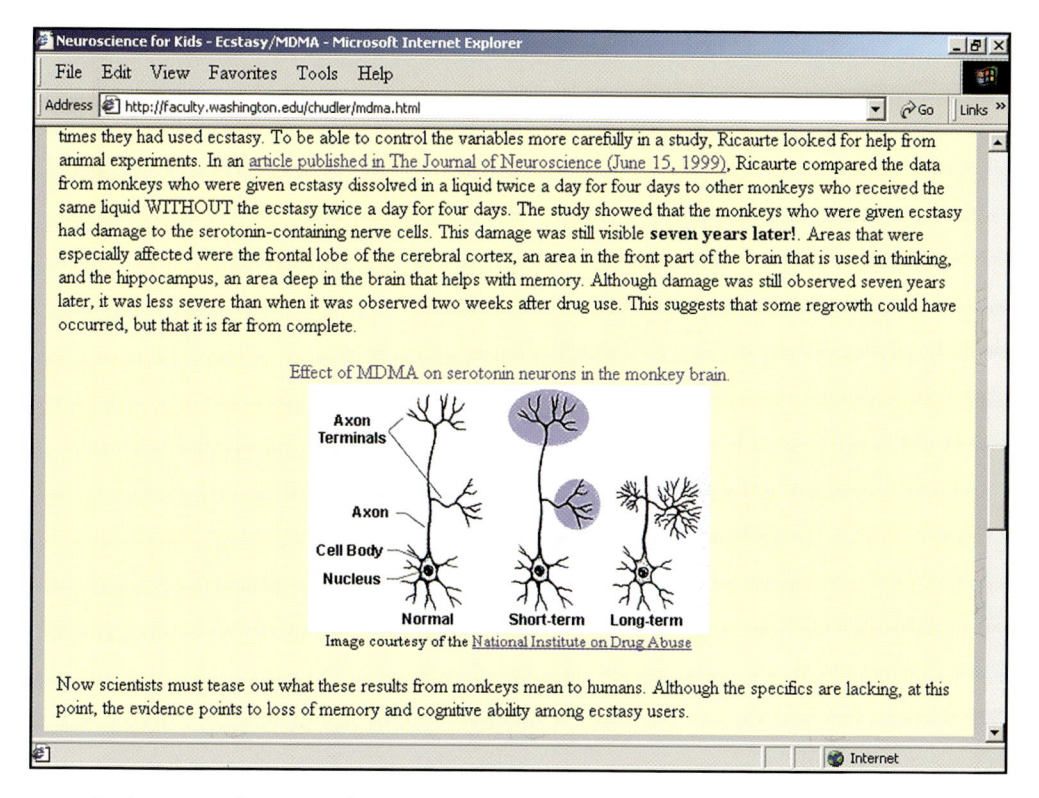

> **Neuroscience for Kids - Ecstasy/MDMA - Microsoft Internet Explorer**
>
> File   Edit   View   Favorites   Tools   Help
>
> Address http://faculty.washington.edu/chudler/mdma.html
>
> times they had used ecstasy. To be able to control the variables more carefully in a study, Ricaurte looked for help from animal experiments. In an article published in The Journal of Neuroscience (June 15, 1999), Ricaurte compared the data from monkeys who were given ecstasy dissolved in a liquid twice a day for four days to other monkeys who received the same liquid WITHOUT the ecstasy twice a day for four days. The study showed that the monkeys who were given ecstasy had damage to the serotonin-containing nerve cells. This damage was still visible **seven years later!**. Areas that were especially affected were the frontal lobe of the cerebral cortex, an area in the front part of the brain that is used in thinking, and the hippocampus, an area deep in the brain that helps with memory. Although damage was still observed seven years later, it was less severe than when it was observed two weeks after drug use. This suggests that some regrowth could have occurred, but that it is far from complete.
>
> Effect of MDMA on serotonin neurons in the monkey brain.
>
> Axon Terminals — Axon — Cell Body — Nucleus
>
> Normal   Short-term   Long-term
>
> Image courtesy of the National Institute on Drug Abuse.
>
> Now scientists must tease out what these results from monkeys mean to humans. Although the specifics are lacking, at this point, the evidence points to loss of memory and cognitive ability among ecstasy users.

▲ *In one study, a control group of monkeys was given saline twice a day for four days while another group was given ecstasy. Two weeks later, scientists saw that most of the ecstasy group's serotonin was gone. Seven years later, the group's serotonin levels were still not as high as the control group's levels.*

Inevitably, young people try to hide their drug problem from their loved ones. Despite their deception, drug abusers give off certain warning signs. Medically, they could experience any of the party-drug side effects mentioned in Chapter 3. MDMA users may give away their secret by storing ecstasy paraphernalia in their room or car. These items include glow sticks, glowing jewelry, angel wings, teddy bears, children's toys, and pacifiers.

In general, drug users tend to become withdrawn, skip class, quit activities, and/or sleep through much of the day. They might ask you to loan them money or just steal it from you. Persistent drug abusers tend to lose weight, look sickly, or seem agitated,

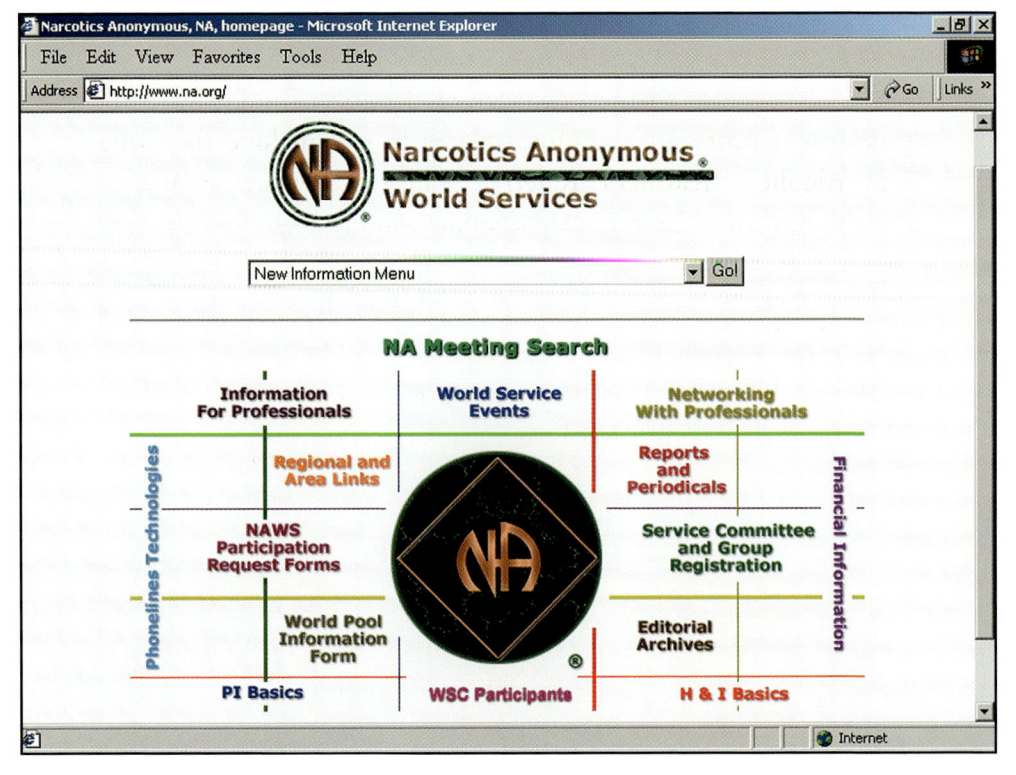

▲ Narcotics Anonymous (NA) is a nonprofit group that holds weekly meetings to help those who are addicted to drugs. As of 2002, NA was holding thirty-one thousand weekly meetings in over one hundred countries.

violent, or depressed. They are in serious need of someone to direct them to professional help.

▶ Where to Go for Help

If you, a loved one, or a friend has a drug problem, you should talk about it with an adult you can trust. This may be a parent, relative, teacher, or doctor. Often it is wise to talk to your school counselor, who is probably trained to handle such matters. Sometimes, though, drug abusers are too ashamed or nervous to discuss their problem with people they know. Help is available for them, too.

Those seeking help with addiction can contact NAADAC, The Association for Addiction Professionals. This organization boasts the nation's largest network of alcoholism and drug-abuse treatment professionals. Other places to call include the Drug & Alcohol Treatment Referral National Hotline, National Helplines, and Narcotics Anonymous. Another helpful organization is the Partnership for a Drug-Free America.

You could also check the phone book. It might list a local drug treatment center, a walk-in medical clinic, or a crisis center. You can call your local library or hospital for advice. Help is available, and it is not hard to find.

Treatment for Addiction

Treatment for party-drug addiction depends on three factors: the type of drug, the extent of the addiction, and the individual. Methamphetamine, for example, is highly addictive. Ecstasy has not been proven to be chemically addictive, but it often causes a strong psychological dependence. People who have been taking drugs for months or years will have a more difficult time going through withdrawal than someone who just started doing drugs. Also, people react differently to drugs. A person who suffers from a physiological disorder (such as clinical depression) or other personal problems may be more dependent on party drugs.

If drug abusers are to beat their addiction, they have to take the first step: admit they have a problem. Drug users then need to commit themselves to what could be a difficult recovery plan. A doctor will determine the appropriate treatment for each patient.

Inevitably, the user will have to stop taking drugs. With highly addictive drugs, this often involves going through withdrawal in a supervised medical setting called detox. People going through withdrawal may have an intense craving for the drug, anxiety, irritability, depression, anger, nausea, shaking, and difficulty sleeping.

Once detox has been completed, the patient needs to go through rehabilitation (rehab) at a drug treatment center. The

MyReportLinks.com Books

▲ *This piece of foil contains methamphetamine powder. Methamphetamine is a highly addictive drug that is difficult to stop abusing once someone starts.*

goals at rehab are to restore a healthy body, improve self-esteem, build family support, and change the individual's behavior and lifestyle. The patient may spend a month or more in rehab. He or she may follow up by joining a support group and/or undergoing therapy to prevent a relapse.

Those with less severe addictions may succeed with counseling and outpatient care. Even for them, recovering from drug abuse is not fun or easy. Former addicts have to grapple with temptation every day. For some, it is a lifelong battle.

▶ Fending Off Predators

When predatory drugs first emerged in the 1990s, unassuming victims were defenseless. In recent years, women have begun taking precautions. Many have purchased date-rape drug test kits, sold online and at drugstores. Moreover, date-rape awareness organizations have formed. Typically, they offer the following advice:

• Do not accept drinks from a man you have not known long enough to trust.

• Opt for drinks that come in sealed bottles.

• Do not leave your drink unattended even for a brief moment. Do not even ask a friend to watch your drink, since he or she might become distracted.

• Watch the bartender pour the drink.

If you feel you have been drugged, you should ask someone to call for an ambulance or drive you to the hospital or a rape crisis center. Also, you should ask to take a urine test as soon as possible. It can determine if a predatory drug such as Rohypnol

PERCENTAGE OF STUDENTS AND YOUNG ADULTS REPORTING PAST YEAR MDMA USE, 1996-2003

Year	8th Grade	10th Grade	11th Grade	12th Grade	Young Students
1996	2.3%	4.6%	4.6%	2.8 %	1.7%
1997	2.3%	3.9%	4.0%	2.4%	2.1%
1998	1.8%	3.3%	3.6%	3.9%	2.9%
1999	1.7%	4.4%	5.6%	5.5%	3.6%
2000	3.1%	5.4%	8.2%	9.1%	7.2%
2001	3.5%	6.2%	9.2%	9.2%	7.5%
2002	2.9%	4.9%	7.4%	6.8%	6.2%
2003	2.1%	3.0%	4.5%	NA	NA

NA = not available
Source: Monitoring the Future Study, Office of National Drug Control Policy

MyReportLinks.com Books

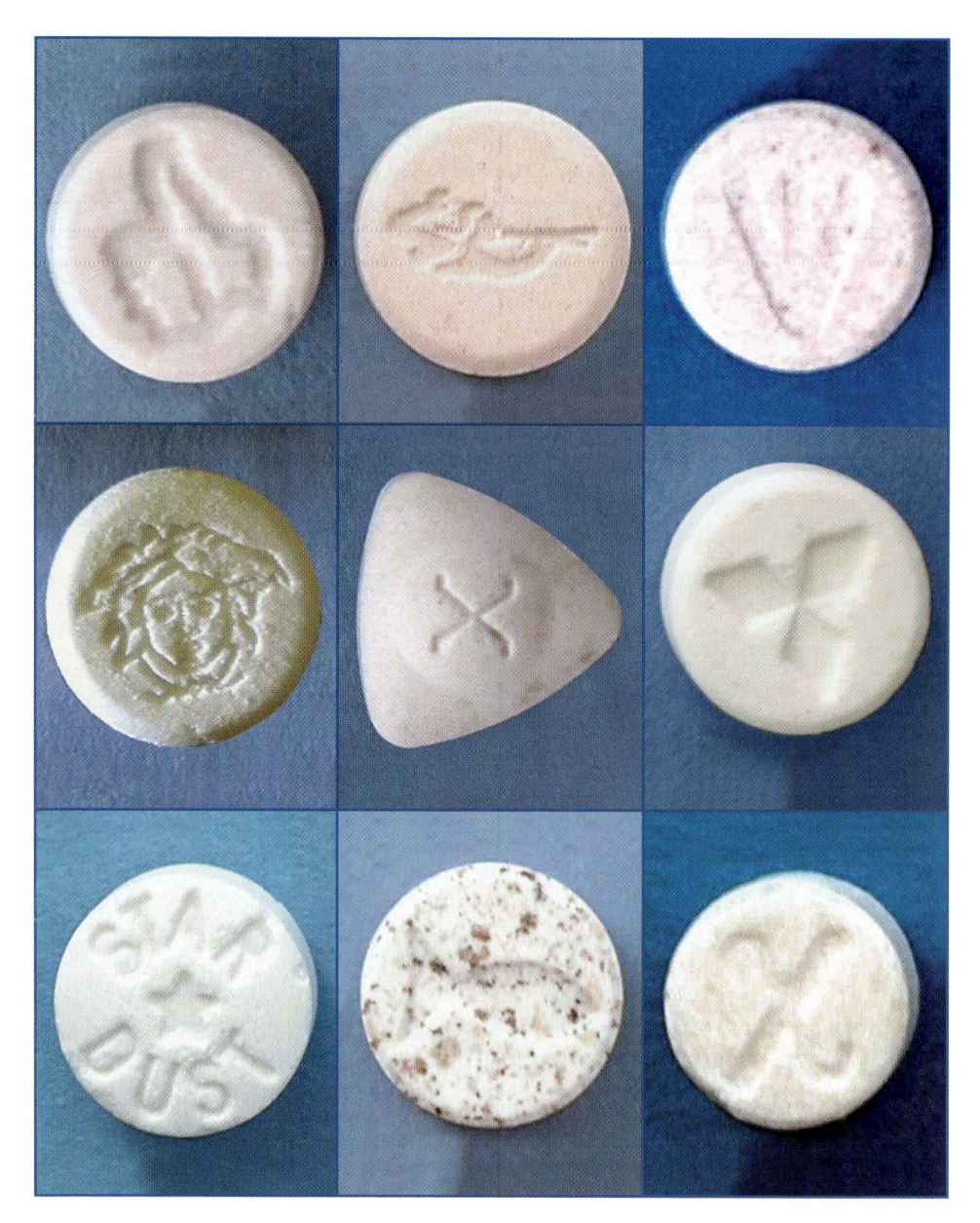

▲ These are just nine of the many different types of ecstasy tablets to watch out for. The people that produce these drugs use interesting brand stamps to make the pills look less harmful than they really are.

▶ 42 ◀

or GHB is in your system; although, sometimes this can be difficult to measure.

Making the Right Choices

In today's world, finding drugs can be easy. They can be found at America's colleges and high schools, and some can be bought on the Internet. If you want to take drugs, you can find a way to get them. However, you owe it to yourself to think about the consequences.

Popping pills may make you feel good in the short term, but where are they taking your life? One ecstasy abuser explained the fate of her drug buddies: "[T]wo have committed suicide, three have moved on to heroin, two have been diagnosed schizophrenic, [and] about six have had to take serious medication or have had complete breakdowns. . . ."[1]

Is that the direction you want to take in your life? Think of your future, your goals, your dreams. Think of all of life's natural highs: in-line skating, skateboarding, swimming, skiing—just to name a few. You can explore new things, go dancing, and joke with friends. You can join clubs or play team sports. Or you can find expression in writing and acting, in music and singing.

The best way to avoid drugs is to avoid the temptation. Stay away from raves and parties where drugs likely will be available. Be wary of "friends" who try to push you into drugs. For most teenagers, drugs are definitely not cool. In fact, more than 90 percent of teenagers do not take drugs. Be proud that you are part of the strong majority. Be proud that you can shove drugs aside and say, "I am better than that."

Do not make the mistake that Lynn made. She had heard that ecstasy was safe and wondrous. She was fooled. "I hear people say Ecstasy is a harmless, happy drug," she wrote. "There's nothing happy about the way that 'harmless' drug chipped away at my life. Ecstasy took my strength, my motivation, my dreams, my friends, my apartment, my money and most of all, my sanity."[2]

Glossary

counterculture—A subculture of society with values that differ from most people.

defibrillation paddles—Electronic devices that use electric shock as a means to restore the rhythm of a heart that is beating irregularly.

dehydration—Abnormally low level of body fluids.

drug paraphernalia—Accessory items that people use to carry, conceal, inject, smoke, or sniff drugs.

drug trafficking—The shipment, sale, and trade of illegal narcotics.

euphoria—Feeling of joy and good health.

hallucination—Perception of the presence of objects that are not real.

manslaughter—The unlawful killing of a person without intention to do so.

morgue—A place where dead bodies are kept until they are identified or released for autopsy or burial.

party drugs—Designer drugs taken and sold at raves, clubs, or other party scenes. They usually are meant to enhance the sights and sounds of the environment.

predatory drugs—Drugs that sexual predators may use to lower the awareness or consciousness of a potential victim.

rape—Unlawful sexual activity conducted against the will of a person by force or threat of injury.

rave—A dance party with bright lights and wild techno music, where party drugs are often used.

serotonin—A chemical in the brain that controls mood, emotion, sleep, and appetite.

Chapter Notes

Chapter 1. The Death of the Party

1. Nicole Hansen, "Real Drugs, False Friends: Nicole Hansen's Story," *drugfreeAZ.com*, n.d., <http://www.drugfreeaz.com/audience/stories_nicole.html> (October 4, 2003).

2. Ibid.

3. Ibid.

4. Ibid.

5. "The Latest Rave," *Flat Rock Forests Unitholder Organization*, n.d., <http://flatrock.org.nz/topics/drugs/latest_rave.htm> (October 5, 2003).

6. Ibid.

7. "A Deadly Trip," *Newshour Extra*, April 11, 2000, <http://www.pbs.org/newshour/extra/features/jan-june00/ghb.html> (October 6, 2003).

Chapter 2. History of Party Drugs

1. "In the Beginning . . . ," *TheDEA.org*, n.d., <http://thedea.org/drughistory.html> (October 10, 2003).

2. Alasdair John MacGregor Forsyth, "A Quantitative Exploration on Dance Drug Use: The New Pattern of Drug Use in the 1990s," *University of Glasgow Faculty of Social Sciences*, November 1997, <http://www.gla.ac.uk/departments/sociology/Phdweb.PDF> (February 19, 2004).

3. *U.S. Drug Enforcement Administration*, February 2003, <http://216.239.39.104/search?q=cache:9gwyfX4KnPUJ:www.dea.gov/pubs/Ecstasy/predatory_drugs-4 .pdf+%22is+by+far+the+most+popular+of+the+party+drugs%22&hl=en&ie=UTF-8> (October 12, 2003).

4. "The History of GHB," n.d., <http://www.test4ghb.com/history.html> (October 13, 2003).

Chapter 3. Effects of Party Drugs

1. Debbie Nevins, "Ecstasy—The agony of the hug drug," *Teen Fad*, February 20, 2002, <http://www.teenfad.ph/news/archives/fture_agonydrug.htm> (October 16, 2003).

2. Ibid.

3. "Lysergic acid diethylamide (LSD)," *Drugs.com*, n.d., <http://www.drugs.com/LSD> (October 19, 2003).

4. Tamar Nordenberg, "The Death of the Party: All the Rave, GHB's Hazards Go Unheeded," *U.S. Food and Drug Administration*, March–April 2000, <http://www.fda.gov/fdac/features/2000/200_ghb.html> (October 21, 2003).

5. "GBL/GBH Drugwatch," *DietFraud.com*, May 11, 2000, <http://www.dietfraud.com/Drugwatch/GBL.html> (October 21, 2003).

6. "'Ecstasy alone can kill': Study," *Yahoo! India News*, September 28, 2003, <http://in.news.yahoo.com/030928/139/282ki.html> (October 23, 2003).

Chapter 4. How Party Drugs Are Made and Sold

1. Donna Leinwand, "Use of 'date rape' drug surges," *USATODAY.com*, January 28, 2002, <http://www.usatoday.com/news/nation/2002/01/28/usat-drug(acov).htm> (October 25, 2003).

2. Lisa Schencker, "New GHB test aims to prevent date rape," *Daily Illini*, August 27, 2002, <http://www.dailyillini.com/aug02/aug27/news/stories/news_story09.shtml> (October 26, 2003).

3. "Remarks of Attorney General John Ashcroft," *U.S. Department of Justice*, September 19, 2002, <http://www.usdoj.gov/ag/speeches/2002/091902operationwebslinglerlg.htm> (October 12, 2003).

Chapter 5. Avoiding Party Drugs, Getting Help

1. "The Latest Rave," Flat Rock Forests Unitholder Organization, n.d., <http://flatrock.org.nz/topics/drugs/latest_rave.htm> (October 5, 2003).

2. "Testimonials from Former Drug Users," drugfreeAZ.com, n.d., <http://www.drugfreeaz.com/audience/college_stories.html> (November 4, 2003).

Further Reading

Dudley, William. *Drugs and Sports*. Farmington Hills, Mich.: Gale Group, 2001.

Espejo, Roman, ed. *Drug Abuse*. Farmington Hills, Mich.: Gale Group, 2002.

Kuhn, Cynthia, et al. *Buzzed: The Straight Dope About the Most Used and Abused Drugs from Alcohol to Ecstasy*. New York: W. W. Norton & Company, Inc., 2003.

Kuhn, Cynthia, Scott Swartzwelder, and Wilkie Wilson. *Just Say Know: Talking with Kids about Drugs and Alcohol*. New York: Norton, W. W. & Company, Inc., 2002.

Lennard-Brown, Sarah. *Drugs*. Austin, Tex.: Raintree Publishers, 2002.

Lindquist, Scott. *The Date Rape Prevention Book*. Naperville, Ill.: Sourcebooks, Inc., 1999.

Littell, Mary Ann. *LSD*. Berkeley Heights, N.J.: Enslow Publishers, Inc., 2001.

Ojeda, Auriana. *Drug Trafficking*. Farmington Hills, Mich.: Gale Group, 2001.

Silcott, Push, and Mireille Silcott. *Book of E: All About Ecstasy*. London: Omnibus Press, 2000.

Weatherly, Myra. *Ecstasy and Other Designer Drug Dangers*. Berkeley Heights, N.J.: Enslow Publishers, Inc., 2000.

Phone Numbers

NAADAC, The Association for Addiction Professionals
   1–800–548–0497

Drug and Alcohol Treatment National Hotline
   1–800–662–4357

National Helplines
   1–800–HELP–111

Narcotics Anonymous
   1–818–773–9999

Index

A
alcohol and party drugs, 29
amyl nitrate, 12, 29
Ashcroft, John, 34

C
"cafeteria-style" drug use, 29
Clark, Dr. Westley, 31
Controlled Substances Act of 1970, 15–16
Controlled Substance Analog Act of 1986, 15
Counterculture, 15
Cutler, Charly, 33

D
designer drugs, 11, 15
detox, 39
Drug-Induced Rape Prevention and Punishment Act of 1996, 16

E
ecstasy (MDMA), 10–11, 12, 15, 17, 21, 22–23, 28, 29, 30–32, 34, 35, 36, 37, 39, 43
ecstasy trinkets, 32
effects, 13, 21–29, 32, 36

F
French, Brandy, 21

G
GBL, 12, 27, 31
GHB, 11, 12, 13, 16, 18–20, 26–27, 28, 29, 31, 33, 35, 43
GHV, 12, 27

H
Hillory J. Farias and Samantha Reid Date-Rape Drug Prohibition Act, 19

I
Internet, 16, 20, 27, 31, 33–34, 41, 43

K
ketamine, 12, 17–18, 24, 28, 31, 32, 35
Kidston, Barry, 15

L
laboratories, 11, 18, 30–31, 35
legal consequences, 25–26, 33–35
London Daily Telegraph, 13
LSD, 12, 18, 24–25, 28, 31, 32, 35

M
methamphetamine, 12, 29, 39

N
nitrous oxide (whippets), 12

P
paraphernalia, 22, 37
Porrata, Trinka, 27
predatory drugs, 11, 16, 18–20, 25–28, 30, 35, 40–41
price, 32

R
rape, 11, 16, 19–20, 25–28, 33–35, 40–41
rave, 10–11, 15, 17, 31–32, 35, 43
rehab, 39–40
Rohypnol, 12, 13, 18, 20, 26, 27–28, 29, 31, 33, 35, 41

S
Schifano, Dr. Fabrizio, 29
Shulgin, Alexander, 17
street names, 20, 22, 24, 28

T
Tarantino, Anthony, 22–23
trafficking, 11–12, 31–34
treatment, 38–40

U
U.S. Army, 17
U.S. Drug Enforcement Agency, 17, 27, 31, 34

W
warning signs, 36–38
where to find help, 38–39

HOMESTEAD H.S. MEDIA CENTER
4310 HOMESTEAD ROAD
FORT WAYNE, IN 46814